Black Woman Surviving:

Passionately Managing My Life

Black Woman Surviving:

Passionately Managing My Life

Author

Dana Martin

Editor

Karissa J. Grant

Dedication

To those we lost. Your lives impacted thousands. You will not be forgotten.

Tysheem Pennock
Suhail Gillard
NaShid Al-Hadi
LaRon Welcome
Diyaan Smith
Justin Porter
David Mitchell
Carlton Price, Sr.
Curtis McKnight

Preface

Hey, y'all! I'm taking a leap of faith and writing about

my feelings, thoughts, hopes, and fears and how they impacted me in 2020. It was hard, but it was a necessary shift in personal perspective. For a long time, I felt alone in how I viewed situations and used my journal to explore my own sense of self, my self-worth, self-awareness, and ultimately my views on the world around me. Look, I'm just a woman trying to figure out all my titles and eke out a space in this strange time. This book is my way of coping with the chaos of the world. Join me as I live my life my own way.

To my reader, this book is a collection of essays about my life in 2020 while being a woman, mother, wife, boss, and teacher. This book is my journey as a black person trying to figure out where I stand. The book is my own story of dealing with COVID-19, a global pandemic and subsequent shutdown, the Black Lives Matter movement, a visceral presidential election, and unyielding gun violence.

Many of us experienced challenges. I'm giving you my

unaltered, raw view of the world through my lens because who am I but me?

This is my 2020 in essays, journal entries, poems, posts,

and lessons I learned along the way. Take this walk with me as I experience 2020 in all its fullness. My hope is that my journey is familiar to some and an eye-opener for others, hell maybe you won't learn anything but

laugh as I fumble my way through the year. It wasn't

pretty for many of us, but I found my way and I hope you did too.

Table of Contents

Introduction

2020 was a lesson and a blessing; the year that brought everything to a standstill. During this time, I found both strengths and weaknesses within myself. I felt unprepared, lost, unable to keep it all together...yet tasked with keeping it all together. I, like so many, ran the gamut of emotions day in and day out.

My life changed.
I grieved life as it was.
I grieved losses.
My heart was
broken. My commute
ended. I lost family.
My roles changed.

I questioned my worth as a wife, woman, mother, and person of color.
I feared dying by virus or violence.
I lost focus.
I gained weight.

I lost relationships.
I cried a lot.
I isolated myself.

I lost my creativity.

I lost my spark for life.

I was scared for days and months on end.

I was drained physically, mentally, spiritually, and emotionally

But I survived.

I looked at my life and realized how full I
actually was.
Then I regained my passion.

I settled into my grown woman.
I rose above for my daughters.
I spoke my inner truth to my husband.
I comforted my sister.
I supported my parents.
I leaned on my friends.
I counseled my students.
I shed the unnecessary.
I regained myself.
My ideas returned.
I figured out that there is no figuring it out.
The lessons just kept coming.

Every single day and instead of fighting against the flow I surrendered to it.

January 2020

"Saying no is one of my greatest self-care tools."

-Dana Martin

Entries

January 3rd: Year of No
January 15th: My Entrepreneurship Journey
January 26th: Live

January 3, 2020

Year of No

Last year was a "year of yes" and this year has turned into my year of no. In 2019, through triumphs and difficulties, I learned a lot about myself. Now I am taking power in limiting myself in what I accept and to which I agree. Truth be told, I feel freer than I have in a very long time. I am preserving my energy for things that I find most important. I tended to spread myself thin, too thin. Many of us do this honestly. We overpromise, while mentally underdelivering. Running around doing a million things and going a million places but producing little substance.

By choosing to say no, I am effectively telling myself that the things I give my energy are what I value. I am taking stock of what drains me and finding ways to end their effect on me. This principle applies in every area of my life — at work, with family, with friends, and in business. I reserve the right to say no to any and everything without guilt, shame, or negative feeling. I have been practicing this mindset and through practice and consistent implementation, I feel more empowered and in control. I am refusing to let outside forces dictate how I live my life and how I feel. Saying no is one of my greatest self-care tools. I use it over and over and guess what y'all? It's working for me.

January 15, 2020

My Entrepreneurship Journey

Here's my story. I'll be honest I have been scared to fully share my story because I was afraid of feeling like a failure in this area of my life. Over the past five years, I have been trying to find ways to earn additional income and become an entrepreneur. I've always had side hustles, but I began accelerating my earnings with the hope of potentially exiting my full-time career. I am an educator by day. The job requires teaching, counseling, and guiding students in the college application and financing processes. It has a heavy emphasis on parents' awareness of financial aid, scholarships, and college choice. I pro- vide direct service and support to all 12th graders and their families as they transition from high school to their next step. There is such a need for direct guidance around college planning for our community (inner city people of color that is), and more parents and students should benefit.

I started to provide individual consultations to those that would contact me outside of my day job. Friends of friends and friends of my students would come to me with additional requests, but I never charged a fee. You see, I'm a helper by nature and didn't feel good about accepting money for the information I shared.

In 2016, I wrote a book, "Creatively Closing the Gap: Unconventional Ways to Find Money for College". I did a modest book tour, gave speeches, and made appearances around my city and in local media. I launched my website and did the legal work, but my dream was not yet realized, as the business didn't produce the profit I was hoping for. I have struggled since the beginning of this journey with balancing being a wife, and mother balancing my physical and mental health. I just can't seem to find the right "formula" to balance everything. Here's how the story would go:

Formula 1:
Turn the hustle up on my business.

Result: My parenting or marriage would suffer. I'd miss a school meeting; my kids would start acting out or my husband and I wouldn't see eye-to-eye.

Formula 2:
Turn up the hustle for business and home.

Result: My full-time job started suffering. It seemed as though my entrepreneurial goals directly competed with my full-time job. This created tension. I started to get ill more often as well. Migraines, strep throat, colds that lasted for months, listlessness, shortness of breath. Everything would catch up to me and beat me down.

Formula 3:

Focus only on my home life.

Result: Everything else would suffer, the business, my 9 to 5, and my social relationships. It's like I couldn't win everywhere at the same time. It became so overwhelming to keep trying and failing in some areas of my life, but there is a fire inside of me for entrepreneurship that will not go away. I have been a part-time party planner for my family most of my life. In the past two years, we had so many parties at our house. It was to the point where I could book all the services needed for a party and have everything together in less than a day. The venue, food, DJ, all services, and decor...done. My kids loved helping with planning and decorating. My husband is good with organization and order. If we love it and we are good at it, why not make money doing it? Together we formed Marty's Parties, LLC, our family business. With our new business, I have had a much easier time balancing this with family. My health has improved tremendously.

So I am here now with both businesses trying to figure out how to push forward. I will continue to promote and set goals, but I feel kind of lost even though I've been at this for a while. In the midst of it all, I am still empowered and inspired to do this work. This is my entrepreneurship story. Straight forward? Not so much, but it's mine and I own it wholeheartedly.

January 26, 2020

Live

Let others know how you feel.
Speak your mind and heart.
Make amends.

LIVE.

There is no tomorrow, only today.
Speak your truth.
Do what you are called to do.

Your life is now, not later. I'm watching how the news of Kobe's death is wreaking havoc on so many. We walk around every day playing small and not realizing this life we are gifted.
LIVE.

LOVE.

Step out on FAITH.

Thank you Lord, for my mind, health, insight, and family. Peace and love everyone.
So much death in these past few months has me reevaluating my life.
LIVE *BIGGER because this life isn't promised.*

February 2020

"I give hard-working women, Black women, working moms, upwardly mobile powerhouses, warrior yet submissive wives, girls with smart mouths, struggling caretakers, little girls who are the smartest in their class, young women who are distracted women who love hard, idealistic but tired women permission to be. Because I am.. because I was.. they can be."

-Dana Martin

Entries

February 5th: Because I am Who I Am
February 16th: Unsettled
February 27th: Free Soul

February 5, 2020

<u>Because I Am Who I Am</u>

"Who does she think she is?"

   "What gives her the right...?" "Why do they listen to her?"

"Why her and not me?"

   "Where does she think she is" "Who's boss is she?"

"She's not even their mom."

     "Why, why, why"

There is so much chatter. Talking behind my back and I hear it, loudly, but you know what - I've questioned myself too. I've asked "Why me?" in all aspects of my life including my marriage, being the mother I am to my girls, my job as an educator, my businesses, my house, my life overall the way I interact with the world.

I know you're wondering, what makes me different? I

show up and do the work, every day. I see a need and do what needs to be done. I don't talk shit and sit back and do nothing. I see what needs to be done and try my best to come up with solutions. I'm not always nice about it. I'm not always cheerful. Hell, I'm not always healthy, but I show up for people continuously. That is more than I can say for so many others.

So with that, the next time someone asks you about me and why I do whatever I do, please tell them because I can and will continue to do so. We need people to get up, show up and do something. That is me. Period.

February 16, 2020

<u>Unsettled</u>

Honestly, I feel crazy today. Do you ever feel like your efforts are just worth nothing? Let me explain. Sometimes it seems like no matter what I do, how I feel, or where I go I don't have an impact overall. I already know how this sounds. Woe is me right? But over the past few weeks, I have felt very ineffective. When I try to speak up about an issue it is quickly pushed aside, or someone tells me that I am wrong for feeling that way. It is frustrating. As a lover of spontaneity who has become an intense by-the-book planner, I am left feeling perplexed. I plan my life so closely nowadays that I tend to know how situations will play out before they begin. Blame motherhood, marriage, and managing hundreds

of students" lives and decisions daily, but I have become

much more straight and narrow than I used to be. Lately, though, the fireside of me has been coming to the surface. I want more; more commitment from others, and more fervor for work. I want more passion and care. Hence the feeling of craze. I guess the saga continues.

Sorry, I'm just having a rough day.

February 27, 2020

Free Soul

What is it about freedom? We want it so badly, but it seems so hard to attain. A truly free soul speaks to your heart in a way that makes you feel invincible. It makes you feel heard. Those souls can't be captured or tamed. They exist outside of our reality only available when we need them most.

I love an honest soul. Someone who is just true to themselves and in turn to you as well. Not necessarily on a romantic level, but on an energy level. Someone with whom you can be free without fear of judgment. A person whose light speaks to you on a plane beyond this physical world. When you are in the presence of someone who encompasses passions with a sense of purpose, who dreams of bigger and turns pain into lessons of resilience that change you. A soul so dope that they give you a perspective that makes you appreciate this life. Someone who is genuinely more real than real. Even when they are hurt, they still emanate a sense of control through inner peace and consciousness. A soul like this can settle a chaotic spirit and can identify a false one.

This energy is not to be taken or used but rather absorbed, harnessed for good, and then released so it can continue to make the world heal. I've encountered this energy in my lifetime and am better for it.

March 2020

"My story, my experiences, and the way I approach the world give my kids permission to be."

-Dana Martin

Entries

March 1st: Why I Do

March 4th: I'm Stretched

March 5th: Still Stressed

March 12th: Who Knows What's Happening

March 16th: Stay at Home

March 20th: Today's Corona Outings

March 24th: Normalcy

March 1, 2020

Why I Do

I serve as a counselor and teacher within a high school. I have 15+ years of experience in college access and youth development. Though the titles are nice there is a much deeper meaning in what I do on a daily basis.

Why I do the work I do:

I want to change mindsets.

I want to help reverse generational poverty.
I want to prevent senseless violence.
I want to overcome despair.

I want to help a parent realize a dream for their child that they don't know how to attain.
I want to end the school-to-prison pipeline.

I want to show my Black and Brown kids endless possibilities.
I want college to save their lives.
I want a goal to give hope.
I want a sport to focus my energy.

I want a career to sustain their lifestyle and provide for themselves and their families.

I want the military to provide discipline for real-life situations.
Exposure.
Opportunity.
Enlightenment.

Giving a damn about our kids.
My kids.
I teach.

I counsel.

I give advice like my kids' lives depend on it.
Do you know why?
Oftentimes it does.

The same college experience, pathway choice, and lifestyle choice you frown upon could have saved that young person's life.
I care about the burden of debt on our Black families.
I care about the Black tax once they "make it".
I worry about the kids I help send to predominantly white institutions that are confronted with racism every day.
I worry about the kids I send to historically Black colleges who can't afford to eat or have excessive loan debt. This is life and death for my kids, your kids, our kids.
I have kids in foster care, two-parent homes, incarcerated parents, and teenage parents who all want better for themselves.

My kids are real people, with real problems in this real life.
Not statistics.

Not a set of data points.
Not GPAs and test scores.
Real people.

I am people-centered. I advise based on the person, their wants, needs, circumstances, and abilities.

We all need to win as a people and I'm doing my part every single day.

Do you want to know why I do what I do?

My kids' lives depend on it.

My life depends on it.

So I'll continue to advise them in hopes of changing their trajectory in some way.

March 4, 2020

<u>I'm Stretched</u>

I ran into a recurring problem a few weeks back. I wanted time away but felt guilty for wanting it. Not time to go on an adventure or time to party. Not time to get all dolled up or even get a massage. I wanted time to be completely alone, with my thoughts doing whatever I wanted (or didn't want) to do. Let me say this before the message is lost. I AM IN LOVE WITH MY FAMILY. All caps to emphasize the feelings lol. My hubby and my kids are my worlds. We spend so much time together. Driving to school, doing weekend activities, cooking together, cleaning together, and joking together. We're legitimately together most of the time and I'm usually fine.

There are times, however, when mommy/wife needs to be alone. Not in a bad way, but in a healthy way. I spend so much time trying to keep the family systems together that when it's time for me I'm depleted. Most of the time when I am by myself I spend it writing, paying bills, or listening to a podcast or audiobook. I spend a lot of my alone time organizing our life. Making to-do lists, organizing calendars, or doing business work. When I am alone I indulge more heavily in my preferred self-care methods (drinking wine or watching Netflix) and I feel absolutely great about it. The true self-care aspect comes with me not being "on" 100%. Time to myself to just not do anything. Uninterrupted, unrushed time to myself without guilt or shame. I see it as taking care of myself so that I can be the best version of myself for them every day at school and at home I'm tired. Man, I need a break.

March 5, 2020

Still Stressed

My job stresses me out. One of my students was killed a few months ago and the constant grief is wearing on me. This year feels harder to help kids make decisions. It's harder for me to make decisions. I'm tired, exhausted mentally and physically. It's hard to come to work and still see this pain on the faces of my students and colleagues.

Trying to reset expectations of learning while we are all still hurting. I took four days off work last week to balance myself. I feel off-kilter. There are so many things that I want to do for myself, but I put myself on the back burner often. I am trying to take intentional steps to improve my mind. I am having trouble getting to sleep at night and trouble waking up in the morning. I have to fold clothes and do things around my house, but cannot muster the focus to do it. I'm trying but trying does not mean it's working. Have you ever felt like this?

Money is one of my fears; running out, not having enough. I want to make plans, but feel like I need money to plan. I feel scared, stuck spinning in circles or running in place. I feel like I just need to get some traction so I can move forward.

Like the cure to how I'm feeling is to get everything done on my list and have enough money to do it and to go on a vacation. I need to get everything done to move forward. But the reality is, I'm stressed so for now I rest.

Have you ever felt like this before? When was it? What was happening in your life? How did you handle this feeling? Talk through your emotions and solution for spiraling this way.

_____

_____

_____

_____

_____

_____

_____

_____

_____

March 12, 2020

Who Knows What's Happening

This feels like a snow day panic. I am packing up my desk and all personal items today because I don't know if we'll be back tomorrow and since it's Thursday I might as well get all my stuff for the weekend. They just announced that Montgomery County, PA is shutting down tomorrow which means half the staff won't be able to come to work.

Everything feels crazy. I'm texting my hubby who's concerned and my oldest who was sent home from her college campus yesterday. Shit's getting real. I doubt they'll shut down schools though. Everything is up in the air. It's like everyone is panicking over the flu. I feel nervous beyond anything else. There's this buzz around the building about a two-week closure. School doesn't close for sicknesses though. Everything just feels heightened and full of uncertainty. Meanwhile, I just want to go home right now.

March 16, 2020

Stay Home

Two-week emergency stay-at-home order in Pennsylvania. I just thought I'd write that in my journal for historical purposes lol.

March 20, 2020

<u>Today's Corona Outings</u>

1.   I found a case of bottled water and bleach spray at the store.

2.   There was no meat at the market.

3.   The liquor stores are boarded up.

4.   I bought fresh fruit from Edible Arrangements because shit's weird right now.

5.   It was 70+ degrees in March and I loved it.

6.   My skin is looking good.

7.   I didn't go completely crazy in the house today.

March 24, 2020

<u>Normalcy</u>

Day 12 and EVERYBODY IS DOING SCHOOL WORK AT THE SAME TIME! Including me! Ok normalcy I see you playa'.

Journal Time - Speak to Me

What is your beginning of the pandemic story? How did the shutdown impact you? Where were you when the world shut down? How did you feel?

_____

_____

_____

_____

_____

_____

_____

_____

_____

_____

April 2020

"I like to be that motivating push. I like to ignite that fire. Even if they think they don't want me to, I like to push until they take off on their own."

-Dana Martin

Entries

April 4th: Motivation

April 17th: You Know What I Miss?

April 28th: My Inspiration

April 4, 2020

Motivation

I strive to say words that are motivating, sometimes harsh, other times kind, but always my truth. Most times people need courage. They know what they need to do. They know how to do it, but they need a push in the right direction. I like to be that push. I like to ignite that fire. Even if they think they don't want me to, I like to push until they take off on their own.

How do I motivate you may ask?
Motivation can look like this:
Giving words of encouragement to take action.
Cheering on the sideline during a challenging feat.
Sitting quietly next to someone as they complete a seemingly difficult task.
Listening while someone tells their deepest dreams and passions.
Helping people realize that they are not alone in their journey.
Telling folks to "tighten up" and stop whining when they get in their own way.

There are millions of ways to motivate. People need to hear how they can do it (whatever it is) so they can believe in themselves.

Being a motivator is its own gift.

Thank you to those I have motivated for helping me realize my potential. and to those who have given me motivation my life is better for it.

April 17, 2020

<u>You Know What I Miss?</u>

Do you know what I miss most about teaching? Being in the presence of students and my peers. The quick judgment calls, the ability to grab a kid in the hallway and remind them to apply for a scholarship, walking toward the front desk and stopping a pre-fight, engaging a parent in the lobby, defusing an escalation with just my presence, asking a kid to go to my office and grab my water bottle, seeing the light in their eyes when they realize how much college actually costs, killing a lesson that took hours to create, singing songs at my desk that only my fellow teachers would understand, hugs and hi-fives, creating real-life memories just because we are at the time in their lives where it matters.

Teaching is not solely about delivering lessons. It's about making an impact. I miss being a force in my building. I miss my kids. I miss my 12th-grade team. I miss my projector. I really miss the energy that comes from walking in a building where despite differences we are all on one accord. We're there for each other. I miss it all. Y'all please remind me of this feeling next year, because we all know this feeling will be long gone!

April 28, 2020

<u>My Inspiration</u>

My mom is the epitome of a matriarch. My mother has always shown me the value of working hard for your family. She keeps everything together in the day-to-day life of my father, sister, her grandchildren as well as for herself. At 67 years old she still takes care of the details large and small, so we don't have to be concerned and this is an attribute that I have gained from her. Our family has been held together by the love and silent sacrifices that my mother has made. Through a mix of stern humor, she guided us through life as lovingly as she knew how giving me that Black mom experience every day.

Our extended family was important to her too and she showed me lasting family bonds which grew my love of gatherings. I fashion the way I show up in the world as a mother, wife, and teacher after her. My mom was a powerhouse educator in our city. Everyone knew her. She taught for 30+ years and received numerous commendations for her work and work ethic. It was never the awards she cherished though. It was the impact she had on the lives of her students that I remember most. She went above and beyond continuously for her students. Not only in the classroom but outside as well.

She always approached teaching as if the students could be her own. As if their parents could be her relatives, her friends. She never talked down about any students or their families because she understood where they came from. She, a first-generation college student from "the hood", had to learn how to navigate the world outside her neighborhood on her own and thus she imparted this wisdom to her students. She taught in the same neighborhoods where she grew up often knowing the kids and their families personally. She was a valued educator. I model my empathy for others and yearn to build a school community from her. As a wife, she dotes on my daddy and gives balance to the two-parent household. She makes everything work. For my sister and I, she has always been there whether we needed her or not. As a daughter, I knew and still know that I can count on her for anything.

I know she will always have my back and that is exactly how I raise my daughters. I will always be their life jacket because I have my own in my mom's. She is funny, yet gracious, hilarious yet traditional, and very much a family-oriented lady. Her style has fashioned the way I live my life and it"s a pretty good life. No words can describe my momma, but hopefully, you get the sense that she's inspired my life in so many ways. Love that lady.

May 2020

"You cannot dictate how someone responds to repeated disregard for their lives."

-Dana Martin

Entries

May 3rd: My Parents

May 10th: Burnt Out No More

May 20th: I just want them to be safe

May 22nd: Scared

May 29th: Enough (Spring 2020)

May 3, 2020

<u>My Parents</u>

Words can never describe what my parents mean to me. For the first time in as long as I can remember I am unable to see my parents whenever I want and it is having an effect on me. I drove to their apartment building today and stood outside. I called them and told them to come to the balcony where I could see them from the sidewalk. It was raining and I didn't care. I cried in the rain outside while telling my parents that I loved them through the phone and aloud. It hurt.

I know how blessed I am to have both able-bodied parents alive and well. I know that their marriage is the foundation that mine stands on. I know that my parenting style comes from theirs. My sister and I wanted for nothing because of them and all of this hit me hard during this pandemic. I missed them terribly. They couldn't pop up at my house whenever they wanted or I to theirs. This shutdown and their age prevented me from seeing two people that are so very important to me. I did not think that it would but it has tremendously. I honestly just want my mommy and daddy.

May 10, 2020

<u>Burnt Out No More</u>

Somewhere along the way, I lost myself. Constantly being on the go and taking care of everyone else has taken its toll on me. But now that I have the time to reevaluate I'm taking action:

Evaluating My Stressors

I'm identifying what stresses me and then developing a plan to eliminate it. The key to this trick is to be as specific as possible. For instance, "money" is a general worry for me, but more specifically budgeting enough money to manage bills, pay the debt, and enjoy our livelihood causes me to panic. Stating the stressor as specifically as possible helps me identify a strategic way to attack that specific worry and not just an ambiguous "money" problem.

Sleep

I have to get enough sleep. My entire mood shifts when I don't sleep enough. I also get sick more often when I'm exhausted. I feel healthier, more alert, and just kinder when I sleep enough. I've definitely been more sleep-deprived over the past few months and it's evident in my life overall and health.

Detox

When I feel better I do better. I'm cleaning out my body

by drinking much more water and eating less meat and more veggies. I'm eating less junk and fried foods and drinking green smoothies with apple cider vinegar.

When my inside is clean I feel good on the outside.

Meditate

Spending time with myself is priceless. I find guided meditations online to listen to. Spotify is my go-to but I also have a personal meditation guru friend who helps me practice mindfulness too.

Loud Music

I blast my music in my car and in the bathroom and get lost. Music takes me to a simpler space and the right songs can relax my mind and mood. Music is transformative and good music heals. I'm using all of these things to jumpstart my transformation back into myself. I was a person before I became Supermom/wife/daughter/sister/entrepreneur/teacher/counselor and everything else. Below are a few other things I am doing to get back to me:

Reading More
Walking Everyday
Writing Daily
Starting Therapy
Dressing Up More Often
Praying More Throughout the Day

Starting now I'm on my journey to getting back to me.

Journal Time - Speak to Me

What do you do to destress? How do you regain your sense of self? List 5 actions you can take when you feel overwhelmed or underwater. You have the solutions to your issues. Let"s start by listing some here.

_____

_____

_____

_____

_____

_____

_____

_____

_____

May 20, 2020
I Just Want Them To Be Safe

I just want my husband to come home safe every day.
I want my dad to be safe out in the world.
I want my cousins to live without fear of being killed.
My daughters to feel safe. My sister. My nephew.
I'm processing but in a heightened state of awareness.

I could be stopped by the police and be killed accidentally on purpose.
Black-on-black crime is not this issue.
Poverty is not this issue.
Victim blaming is not this issue.

Showing respect and compliance is not this issue.
Good cop, bad cop is not this issue.
Power. Institutional Racism. White Privilege. Living in a country that values money over lives and continuously shows us - is the issue.
Being who I am, is a threat.

By just being a black man - He is a threat.
But we matter.
We've protested loudly and silently. We've marched. We've acclimated. We've assimilated. We've been educated, and yet we still go unheard.

Violence is the only thing that gets attention. The revolution will be televised. You cannot dictate how someone responds to repeated disregard for their lives.
I am tired, unsettled, and in a constant state of fear for my loved ones and myself.

60

We are tired.

Be on the right side of this because a change is coming. I feel it.

May 22, 2020

Scared

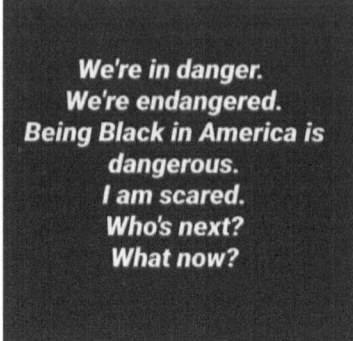

Post from May 2020

You know I'm scared of my husband wearing his black mask at work and in that particular neighborhood?

I'm scared of him walking to get lunch and being wrongly accused of anything.

I'm scared for him on many occasions. Just because he's a Black man in a world not built for him.

May 29, 2020

<u>Enough (Spring 2020)</u>

I am feeling overwhelmed on so many levels. The fear of becoming ill and the world shutting down this spring due to the global pandemic affected me deeper than I thought. Even before this pandemic, I took time off work because I was mentally stretched. I was tired and unfocused and confused. I felt like I was operating in a fog. I couldn't get myself together. Maybe my mind and body were preparing me for a shift.

I am tired. I'm tired of being tired. These past few days, weeks, and months have worn on my soul. Worn on my very being. I have been trying to release each thing only to be hit by something else soon after. This pandemic has made me reevaluate my sense of self. I am a people person. I am good in person. I am not an online instructor. Technology has scared me for a very long time. I am completely out of my comfort zone. I am also failing at being a good home teacher for my baby girl. Her sleep schedule is completely off, she's not actively engaging in classwork or Zoom meetings and I feel like I just can't fight with her. I also see how hard staying in the house is for her. Not being around her friends and being active. I feel like I am failing to keep her educated, engaged, active, and learning.

My students are struggling to stay engaged. I feel so incredibly sad about the end of the year. I reign over this part of the year. I get so much joy and satisfaction from organizing graduation, senior week, college decision day, and all of the end-of-year events for our seniors. Curating memories that will impact the rest of their lives. I feel like my kids were robbed. I went into full-blown mourning when they announced that school was over for the rest of the year. I didn't realize how much meaningfulness and self-worth I tied to the end of the school year and all the special moments. I had to set aside time for myself to deal with the emotions I had around all of it. Mrs. Martin represents all of that.

In the midst of all this one of my closest students got in a car accident after picking her brother up from college. She was seriously injured and he was killed in the crash. It was 9 AM on a Saturday the day before the Islamic celebration of EID. They weren't doing anything wrong. They both were college kids. Raised in a two-parent home. A family that reminded me of mine so much. I told her frequently that her mother was one that I aspired to be like. We ran into her and her mom at Target on our wedding anniversary and talked for a while. I always admired her mother and how close their family was. When I got the phone call all I could think about was her and then her parents. I know how we value our family. The life that we want for our kids. We make all the "right" decisions so that our kids can be safe and give them the life they deserve. We move to the #right"

neighborhoods, put them in the #right" schools, put them

in activities, and support them in all decisions, good and bad. We work hard at our jobs to give them good examples and have a loving healthy marriage to model for them. And an accident can take one of our kids away in a flash. It is so unfair. For everyone. My heart literally broke talking to her at midnight while she lay in the hospital alone. She was broken and I was broken for her and her entire family. I felt and still feel awful. At the balloon release, I watched my husband tear up thinking about what it's like as a father to lose a son. I watched him see himself in her father as he talked about the bond, life, and legacy of his 23-year-old son. We both recognized ourselves in her parents and that made the mourning so much harder. This grief is sadness and sympathy for her and her entire family. They are a regular upwardly mobile Black family just like ours. It hurts. In the midst of all this, Black people keep getting killed with force. I'm tired. It's mentally stressful. I'm scared about it. The civil unrest in the country is a symptom of years of racism. I'm tired. I'm scared for my husband. I'm constantly worried about his interactions with white people at work and in the surrounding affluent neighborhood. He's a tall black man with a straight face that is now required to be partially covered with a mask and I worry about that mask all the time. If one person sees him as a threat to their existence they can shoot him, hurt him, or call the police on him because they feel threatened and he is simply there to do his job. I don't feel safe for him. I'm constantly upset about it. I'm scared all the time for him. I worry about his mental health under those conditions. I worry about him snap-ping one day as the micro-aggressions pile up. I'm just tired of all these emotions. People are tired of feeling scared. Looting is a symptom of a bigger problem. We are threats just by our existence. I'm tired of talking about it. Tired of explaining it. I'm worried about and for my daughters. I'm physically tired from the emotional strain. It seems like there isn't anything that we can do to make a change. I want change but don't know how to. Nobody is coming to save us. We have to figure it out. I feel a shift. These protests feel different. It's all too much, but yet not enough.

June 2020

"I've heard people say "Why can't people be more like Martin Luther King?" I say what's the difference, they killed him too."

-Dana Martin

Entries

June 1st: Sick and Tired

June 5th: Busy

June 10th: Open Letter to My Seniors

June 30th Feel Like Civil War is Coming

June 1, 2020

Sick and Tired

> Aren't yall tired? Because I am. Tired of being scared. Living fearfully. Tired of feeling powerless. Tired of waiting for the next name. Tired of wondering if it will be someone I know. Racism is so alive.

Post from June 2020

I'm so tired of being angry. People just aren't getting it. I am TERRIFIED for my husband, father, nephew, and every Black male figure in my life. It shouldn't be this way. Honestly, I'm terrified for myself. This feels like some kind of police state; a country on the verge of a civil war. I am literally at a loss for what to do now. I pour my life into my family and my profession trying to create positive opportunities for people to see their purpose.

How can I combat this plague of deadly violence from law enforcement toward our Black men and women? You can say all of the "he should or shouldn't have done this or that" but at the end of the day "to protect and serve" is a motto not reserved for us. How can things be better? I really feel like I (or my family) could be next and this feeling just won't go away. I don't know what to do.

June 5, 2020

Busy

Random thought - trash hasn't been picked up in what feels like months. I noticed because I've made myself busy. I'm constantly cleaning and throwing things out

and the trash keeps piling up higher and higher. The family business has far exceeded expectations during this pandemic. We have orders almost daily. People want to celebrate their loved ones and we are obliging as safely as possible. It also gives us something else to focus on rather than this virus, virtual school, police brutality, gun violence in Philly, and all else negative. I poured myself into my work to celebrate my students this year. This particular class of 2020 has dealt with so many heartaches and hardships. I poured myself into making sure they at least felt celebrated. In this time of closure, I'm finding myself driving around a lot. I drive to pick up helium, deliver balloon orders, and pick up groceries. There always seems to be something to do, somewhere to go. I'm wearing myself thin and I'm supposed to be at home. Time to reset something. - Wait, do I hear a trash truck? Aww, shucks now!

June 10, 2020
<u>Open Letter to my Seniors: You Matter!</u>

This school year has been hard. One of our seniors lost her mom. We lost a beloved student to gun violence. Many of you lost loved ones. We lost the end of the school year. We lost prom. We lost graduation. We lost celebrations. A virus took so much away. Racial trauma is continuing to plague us. Over and over again. I'm angry, sad, anxious, fearful and so tired. Tired of everything.

I do the work I do because you need someone to speak for you. You need an advocate, someone in your corner. I worked hard to secure my position, mastered my craft, built a reputation, and gathered connections so I could be a resource for my people. My youth. My students. My kids. You. College advising is a way for me to help you realize you are bigger than your surroundings. A way to help you realize your dreams. A way to help you realize that you can do anything you want in this life. A way to visualize your future. Sometimes it involves convincing you to do things you don't want to do. It's about being a presence in your lives. Someone that's in your corner even if you don't know it. I advocate. All the time. Sitting on the phone with colleges, recruiters, and scholarship committees, writing letters to appeal boards, and driving busloads of Black kids across the state to see college campuses, but aside from college I do this every day for my kids. I show up. I stand tall for you by just being myself. I'm a Black educator on purpose. My being present represents more than just a job. My kids come to me to cry, parents ask me to console them, and I talk to you, my students like you are my own children, I hold you accountable, and I fight for you behind the scenes all the time because if I don't who will? That's how I approach it. You deserve to be kids. You deserve support. You deserve your playing field to be leveled. I call myself a College Advisor Mom for a reason. I feel like I'm saving lives every day by just being here.

At the same time, I am hurting to my core. Black people keep being killed as if our lives don't matter.
George Floyd.
Breonna Taylor.
Ahmaud
Arbery.
Trayvon Martin.
Tamir Rice.
Sandra Bland.
Armando
Castille. Eric
Garner.

Sean Bell.
Oscar Grant.
Mike Brown.
Walter Scott.

I'm scared all the time that someone I love will be on this list. I'm scared for my husband, my daughters, and my entire family. Scared for you, my students. There isn't a time that I am not scared. It's not fair. I don't want to personally know the next name on the list. It's not fair that we must live our lives like this. In constant fear. In a war state.

I've had a gun pulled on me twice in my lifetime. Once I was walking down the street and I fit the description of someone who robbed a 7-Eleven. The police pulled guns and ordered me to put my hands up. The second time I was in bed asleep. The police ran into the house looking for a suspect. I was in bed. They kicked in the bedroom door and drew guns. If I would have moved or been defiant or perceived disrespectful, I could have been killed. I could have been Breonna Taylor. That realization frightens me.

We fight for good schools, we fight for opportunities, we fight for jobs, we fight for resources, we fight for our health, we fight for respect, and we fight every day for our lives and it's not fair. I draw strength from doing the work. It feels like a calling to pour my energy into something positive especially if nothing else is in my control. I can inspire change. I can be the change. My children and you, my kids are the future and I sacrifice and pour into you so that you can stand a fighting chance. I'm angry. I'm hurt, but we as a people will rise above. This movement, this energy there is a shift happening. You are living during a time in history that will be written about. This is a revolution on so many levels.

I am a Black woman. Wife. Mother. Sister. Friend. Daughter. Teacher. Counselor. Mentor. So many titles, but none of them mean anything. Above all I am a person, a human being whose life matters. I matter to those who know and love me just as they matter to me. I am a Black educator on purpose. My story, my experiences, and the way I approach the world give you, my kids, permission to be. Through all this tragedy we as a people will make it through.

Keep fighting. Keep pushing. Don't give up no matter how hard it gets. There are more people who love you and are rooting for you in the background.

The time for change is now.
With love,

Mrs. Martin

Journal Time: Speak to Me

Imagine a time in your life when you wanted to share how passionately you felt for a cause. Write a letter to that someone. Describe the cause and your feelings. Write now!

_____

_____

_____

_____

_____

_____

_____

_____

_____

_____

June 30, 2020

Feels Like A Civil War

It feels like a war is brewing. Everything on my timeline is about Black Lives Matter. Names keep filling my screen. There are more protests now than in the past 100 years calling for racial justice asking that our people not be murdered at the hands of the people sworn to serve and protect. It feels like people in my immediate circle get it. My friends, family, and some coworkers get it, though not all. It seems that those I follow on social media get it, though not everyone. I live in Philly. A big city with big city ideals and issues. A city where people openly criticize the utter gaw of the current president. People call his judgment into question frequently in places I frequent. It's normal here, but many if not the majority of people within our country feel completely different from the way I do about respecting black lives and the need to defend them. Many support the policies and rhetoric of the current administration, the thinly

veiled bigotry paraded as #law and order", immigration

attacks, and the way in which the 45th president engages with and speaks about people of color. Many do not believe that racism has an impact on lives daily. Many do not believe in white privilege and the benefits that have been granted unknowingly. The oblivion that exists is vast and scary.

I believe that there will be a civil war in this country in which race will play a particularly notable role. I feel the tension whenever a system is pushed. Whenever someone questions the police. Whenever police brutality is explained away as a necessary force. Whenever someone shouts "all lives matter" in response to Black Lives Matter. As if we have the audacity to claim that Black lives matter in a way that usurps their freedoms. As if saying that the mattering of the lives of Black people takes away anything from anyone. Whenever respectability politics are brought up in response to the deaths of George Floyd, Sandra Bland, Oscar Grant, Freddy Grey, Tamir Rice, and Trayvon Martin it sickens me.

To say that these individuals would not have been killed if they had complied, been kind, been submissive, or done what the officer said is a contradiction to the very fabric of our nation. I say well what about Breonna Taylor, Atatiana Jefferson, and Botham Jean who were killed in their own homes by police? What about when people weaponize the police against Black bodies like Christian Cooper? or even Mike Brown, Eric Gardner, and Alton Sterling who were suspected of committing a crime? Is it ok to kill them? Where is that in the Constitution? Protect and serve? Law and order? Innocent until proven guilty? Where? For Black folks? I think not. How about this? If someone is committing a crime, arrest them, don't kill them. That's what the criminal justice system is about right? Why is it fair to assume that if someone who is

Black is not following rules it is acceptable for a law enforcement officer to kill them? Now I understand the intricacies, fallacies, and misdoings of the criminal justice system and have had plenty of people that I hold near and dear become victims of said system, but they are still alive. We are asking for a basic right. Don't kill me because you're scared and I'm Black. The heightened fear around black skin is so real it frightens me.

Here in Philadelphia this week a group of white men and women stood guard in front of a statue of Christopher Columbus with rifles as a show of protection. These people were called patriots and there was little to no police interference. I thought that if their skin color had been darker the outcome would have been different, dangerously different. The narrative would have been vastly different. Multiple arrests would have been made; blood likely shed. I'm sick of the double standard, but it does not surprise me. It doesn't surprise me when coworkers express their disdain for the looting and burning, proclaiming that "blue lives matter," but are silent about the reasons people are standing up in the first place. They are critical of the revolution and the aftereffects, but not of the racist system that has killed, imprisoned, and otherwise disadvantaged countless Black people. This is not about all lives. This is not about all people. This is also not about Black-on-Black crime. This issue is about police brutality and how it is acceptable to kill Black people when they get out of line because we are deemed inferior.

The pandering is bothering me as well. I don't want to be racially profiled and potentially murdered by the police. I want that to stop. I don't need or want emails and commercials from every company I have ever patronized about how great Black people are. A day off for Juneteenth? Great. "Black is beautiful" beer? um ok. Martin Luther King crab legs? sure. Reparations rum punch? I'm not here for all of that. I just don't want the system to be against me or to kill my loved ones. Got it?

Why should Black people shoulder all of the effort to explain why Black Lives Matter? There is no way someone who does not believe in my worth as a person will listen as I try to explain the value of Black lives and how systematic racism is affecting our entire country. I don't mean anything to them. I'm just a Black woman with an agenda. I'm one of them loudmouth, big lip stupid n...ers. I can't stand up to someone who doesn't see my value. If people have a belief that Black people are inferior whether blatant or implicit then documentaries and movies can not help. They will not engage in that material. This work is two-fold. There are places I can not go because I am not welcomed due to the color of my skin. Not outright of course, but implied.

There are counties and dinner tables and country clubs and shore houses and mountain houses that are not places for me and I know it. You know it. I am not wanted and do not belong. I can not infiltrate these places with my logic speaking of equality and equity for Black people. My allies can though. This is the time in which anyone who supports the message of Black Lives Matter can speak to those who look like them and help bring about real change.

Conversation.

Understanding.

Or at least make a stand in the face of racism.

I do see people wearing thin. The lady in Central Park who called the police on the Black man to weaponize blue against Black, the lady who painted over the Black Lives Matter mural in California with her sidekick

screaming "All lives matter" and "We're sick of Black

Lives Matter", the Trump rallies full of hate, the political commercials antagonizing the defunding of the police campaign. Many people want this to go back to "normal." There is a want for this all to "die down", for the Black Lives Matter folks to stop being so radical. Some believe that it's safer when everybody is kind and calm and not protesting and just smiles and nods. People are tired of being called out for their racist behaviors especially when they didn't perceive themselves this way in the first place. They didn't know. They shouldn't be punished. I see the hesitation when people are engaging with people of color. People do not like being identified as racist. People do not like having their views judged. There is a silent majority not making waves either way. Just staying silent hoping this too blows over. Like the 1992 LA race riots, like the 1964 Philadelphia race riots, like the Civil Rights era protests, like the sit-ins, like every other time that Black people have stood their ground it has gone away eventually, but this feels different. Change is necessary and now is the time.

I've heard people say "Why can't people be more like Martin Luther King?" I say what's the difference, They killed him too. What's the difference in the Black Lives Matter approach? If your life or the lives of your loved ones were being threatened by those meant to protect you wouldn't you do whatever was in your power to stop them? I really don't think critics of the Black Lives Matter movement understand what is taking place. This time feels different. It feels like there are clear sides and people are taking a stand. Be ready.

It feels like a civil war is coming.

Journal Time: Speak to Me

Take a second to breathe. Oftentimes we experience heaviness without reflection. Reflect on the thoughts expressed above. How are you impacted by the views shared? Do you remember what you felt like in June 2020? Did your community experience racial uprisings? Did this have an impact on you? Reflect below.

_____

_____

_____

_____

_____

_____

_____

_____

_____

July 2020

"It is a perceived notion that you must be perfect all around, and have a perfect image everywhere so that you can advise. My question is how can people grow if the mistakes they make are continuously used against them?"

-Dana Martin

Entries
July 7th: My Oldest, My Love
July 14th: Missing You
July 20th: Who's to Judge?
July 22nd: My Little Baby
July 31st: Breonna Taylor

July 7, 2020

My Oldest, My Love

Let me tell you what she means to me. When she was in 2nd grade we worked on a school project for hours. It was some kind of diagram with grass and stones and was in a really big box. She was so happy to be working on this project and with me. I remember worrying that the cat would tear up the project overnight so I stayed up all night in the living room to make sure that didn't happen.

In the morning she took the big box on the school bus as happy as she could be. I vowed during that time in our relationship that I would marry Daddy so that we could continue to share moments like this. I wanted to be a partner with her mom in being a women role model in her life. I never realized how much I needed her to be a part of my life. She has taught me so much about myself. I have always taken care of people, but she is different. Her compassion for people and willingness to love and be loved is admirable. I have grown as a person with her in my life. I can honestly say that I am a better person since being able to share her as a daughter.

My world is forever changed because you are a part of it. This year my kid started a business and then another, and she's still in college. She never ceases to amaze me. These things may seem ordinary, but I am in awe of a teen who can manage during this extreme time of uncertainty and civil unrest. She is a protester in her spirit and has marched in support of many causes including the Black Lives Matter movement. She is an advocate for those who need a voice, but this movement is different. It impacts all of us personally. She is doing what she can to ensure that she is a good example for her younger siblings. That she makes her three parents proud. That she has something for herself in the future. We worked so hard to lay a foundation for her, one in which she can spread her wings and fly. We were honestly scared when her school shut down and she had to complete the rest of her freshman year online, but she prevailed. Took summer classes and took up two trades. She didn't lose hope.

She keeps pushing forward and that is what I want for all young people but especially mine. She could have given up but she didn't. Uncertain times, tragedies, and heartache all came this year but she kept pushing forward. She's a real one. I'm proud to be in her corner because she's going far in this life. She has no idea but she's going to change the world somehow. I'm betting on it.

July 14, 2020

Missing You

I miss you.

The way you walked.
Your posture.
You're facial features.

The way you wore your clothes.
Your demeanor.
How tough you were.

Your smart mouth and sly jokes.

The excitement in your voice when speaking of your
talents.
Your love of your craft.
Your eyes.
The way your face lights up to music.
Your love of Black people.
Your growth.
Your ambition.
Your sense of humor.

The fire that burned brightly inside.
You're spontaneity.
I miss you. Dearly.

Because somehow you become a stranger.

A person is gone.

And this stranger is someone I know.
And it is me.
I miss me.

July 20, 2020

Who's To Judge?

People put so much emphasis on perfection when speaking of Jada Pinkett-Smith and public figures in general. I think about all the critics saying she can't be an expert on interpersonal relationships or give advice through channels like the Red Table Talk because of her recent admission of infidelity in marriage. She is a human being. That is one thing that has frightened me throughout my professional journey. People believe that if you fail in one aspect of your life then you don't have the right to give advice on any topic in life. People are trying to cancel her because of this new revelation. It is a perceived notion that you must be perfect all around, and have a perfect image everywhere so that you can advise. My question is how can people grow if the mistakes they make are continuously used against them?

One reason I have not fulfilled many of my passions publicly is that I am fearful of people's reactions to mistakes I have made in the past and how that would affect their opinion of me in my new endeavors. I empathize with Jada. I do not know the intricacies of her marriage.

I don't know her personally nor do I know much about her personal life. I know that I appreciate her perspective on many issues and I do value what she has to say about her personal experiences. People can choose to agree or disagree, but I personally have an issue with "cancel culture" as we all are one mistake away from alienation. That culture demonizes people for decisions they've made in their personal life that may be contrary to their public persona.

It's frightening for me as a woman who sometimes has a small public platform, but oftentimes has the ear of people. To think that if one perceived misstep is revealed all good deeds will go undone is tragic. We as a people do not give grace. Many times we are judged by our worst as opposed to the sum total of our good deeds. We are judgmental creatures by nature. I just wish that more grace were given especially in situations where you do not have a personal stake. It's hard for people to be in the limelight especially when folks are waiting to tear you down.

July 22, 2020

<u>My Little Baby</u>

Throughout this whole crazy year, my baby girl has stayed consistent. She has faced a global pandemic like the rest of us and lost her ability to go to school and be with friends and family, but she has been managing as well as the rest of us. She was supposed to have a big party for her 10th birthday this year and this shutdown has changed all of our plans, but she is still moving gracefully. She says she wants to be an actress, a comedian, or a teacher. She is the ultimate people person. She likes to be around people and make them laugh, but she also likes to organize and be in charge. She likes to have company and friends and for people to be on one accord.

That"s her.

My Tink Tink. My deep thinker and empath. She cares so deeply about so much, and that is why I worry about her and all she is absorbing in this crazy world right now. I know that she will care for me if I ever need it. Her heart is so big. Her personality is big and bright. I just want so much for my baby girl. She has adapted to this changed sense of normal with no notice and little hesitation. Yes, there was fear and anxiousness as we all tried to figure out our way during the school year, but there was so much more time to spend together that we cherished.

I learned just how she learns in the classroom by observing her work ethic on the computer. I learned who her school friends are and the types of conversations they have. I learned what she values as a little person and what she worries about. I love that she still clings to innocence and asks me questions hourly. She wants to be read to even though books are mommy's thing as she says. She is incredible and this year I had the ability to turn off the unnecessary and pay attention to this person that is blossoming in front of me. I love her but more so I adore how she is growing. I'm paying more attention and I am loving what I am seeing.

July 31, 2020

<u>Breonna Taylor</u>

It's still unbelievable, or not. This happens often. The

perception of guilt because of our blackness, the company we keep, and the communities we live in. Shooting her is justified because the no-knock warrant was the law. It's justified because the police officers were shot at by her boyfriend in the dark, in the middle of the night. Even though Breonna and her boyfriend were at home asleep, and someone barged into their home unannounced. Even though her boyfriend was licensed to carry. Let's be clear, they weren't doing anything wrong. They were asleep. You know because when you have work in the morning, you go home, where you are safe and can rest for the next day's work.

It's taken for grant ed. White people, people that are not from working-class communities, and communities not of color can take this for granted. This is not an anomaly. It is the law and her life does not matter as much as someone with more prestige, less melanin, or more money. I'm hurt that I am not surprised by any of this. Breonna Taylor should not be a hashtag. She did absolutely nothing wrong. She was asleep in her own house and the police came in and shot her.

Atatiana Jefferson was shot and killed by the police while in her home playing video games with her nephew. AT HOME! Your home is supposed to be your sanctuary. Sleep is supposed to be your refuge, but the cops shot them and justice has not been served because Black skin doesn't matter, and being a woman doesn't get respect. Add socioeconomic status and you might as well be invisible. Forgotten. Fucked over. Unprotected. "Shoot first and ask questions last. That's how most of these so-called gangstas pass," but what if the gangstas have the law on their side? Her life doesn't matter to the masses. Just one more death in the saga of the disrespectful treatment of Black women by a society that fails to see our equal worth and find justifications for our mistreatment. I am a Black woman from Philly. Three times a threat or three times more likely to be dismissed, disrespected, forgotten, and unprotected. Unfair, but not likely to change. I'm fearful for my daughters. I'm fearful for myself.

July's theme is the love of Black women. How can you express your gratitude, protection, and love for Black women in your daily life?

_____

_____

_____

_____

_____

_____

_____

_____

_____

_____

August 2020

"So many of us struggle with the Superwoman syndrome, but that day I felt 100% helpless."

-Dana Martin

Entries

August 1st: His Wife
August 14th: Panicked
August 25th: Crossroads

August 1, 2020

His Wife

Writing about him is hard. I look at him with awe and wonder sometimes. Marriage is glorious, loving, hard, unpretty, and messy work. It can be taxing. It can be boring, but it's work to put yourself aside for someone else. To merge your life with another. I love my husband, simply. We've been working to make it and it shows I appreciate him. Becoming a better wife has taught me a new level of patience. To take someone else into consideration. I am not always right. He's not always right. It is not always one way of doing things. You can show love differently. You have to be willing to listen without a response ready and be willing to try. Try hard all the time.

I always loved my husband but was selfish and unkind. I thought I knew everything. I thought I had to be right all the time and have all the answers. Marriage is hard because it is work. He taught me that I do love and can love in a way that is unselfish. I don't have to be in control of everything and that is ok. Every day I wake up feeling like I need him more and more by my side. I admire the man he is, the father he is, the husband he is, and the protector. He helps me continuously believe in myself and my abilities and I am thankful for that. In the past, though I'd be grateful for him, at times it didn't feel like we were a team. We are a stronger team now.

A team against the world and I am amazed at how he continues to show up for me. Not just for the kids, but for me. He has the power to change my mood. To change my mind. He listens to me more now. He makes me feel important to him and I want to do this marriage thing for as long as we can. Throw a pandemic in and you get everything at once. Do we argue? Yup. Do we disagree? Absolutely, but we regroup and do it again. Being stuck in the house together taught us how to be together better.

August 14, 2020

Panicked

Panic and anxiety. That was all I felt. For a four-hour period, I experienced one of the most mentally debilitating experiences of my life. Never would I have ever thought that I would have a panic attack, but I did. It wasn't the textbook panic attack that people hear about. I was actually out in the world interacting with people, even driving. I started to feel an overwhelming sense of anxiety as I was leaving my house. The sense grew bigger and bigger, wrecking me with thoughts of over- whelm and physiological signs of distress. Hotness in the face, difficulty breathing, inability to concentrate. I sent my husband a text saying that I was in the midst of some kind of anxiety attack while driving on the highway.

During this episode, I was still able to function in the world which above all else made me the saddest. I drove, greeted people, and saw my parents. I acted and functioned "normally" but the entire time I felt overcome. I couldn't place the root of the emotion until much later when I finally burst into tears once I got back home. The saddest thing for me was being able to "function" without anyone knowing what was really going on. I was scared to death in the midst of it all. I employed all of my calming techniques and tricks but did not let anyone on the outside know that I was struggling inside. How many people go through life like this? I was eventually ok. I talked it out. wrote it out, slept it out. Then began my search for a new therapist. The fact that I could hide the level of pain and discomfort I was experiencing so well was a wake-up call for me. I know so many of us struggle with the Superwoman syndrome, but that day I felt 100% helpless. The best thing I could do then and can now do for myself is to practice effective personalized self-care. I totally made that term up but it applies. I need to adhere to my own self-care regime and that's whatever works for me. The lessons for me in this were:

1.   Love yourself enough to be and seek the help you need.

2.   Have compassion. You never know what someone is going through on the inside.

3.   These same lessons keep coming back. I need to learn them before I am undone.

August 25, 2020

<u>Crossroads</u>

I feel like I'm at a crossroads in my life. I have cut ties with many people, some for good, some not so good. My daily routine is drastically different. I am no longer on the go. Staying home has slowed me down considerably. I am having a hard time wrapping my head around whether or not I am a success. I can look at someone else's life and help them realize all the success they have. Success in family, love, health, and life overall, but when it comes to me, I get stuck. I value what and whom I have, but I feel like I live for them, every day. I can visualize their goals and set plans to make them happy.

I put my own plans by the wayside. No one else does it, just me. I see to-do lists that I write week after week, month after month that show I put myself to the side, but I ensure that my loved ones get exactly what they need. I'm good at filling the gaps, making sure others are cared for so well that they don't even notice, yet I don't hold myself to the same standard. I need to find a way to hold myself accountable. To finish the tasks that are important to me and to accomplish items on my seemingly endless to-do lists. I need a breakthrough. I have to create my own breakthrough and unstick myself or I'll continue with these same ole patterns.

Journal Time: Speak to Me

Have you ever felt this way? Stuck yet in your own way?
Write about that time here.

_____

_____

_____

_____

_____

_____

_____

_____

_____

_____

September 2020

"Be kind to yourself, educator. You cannot face this world ready to tackle the perils of COVID-19, racism, police brutality, gun violence, and virtual learning for your students and your own family on an empty tank."

-Dana Martin

Entries

September 2nd: Self Care For Educators
September 15th: A Forever Battle
September 26th: Breonna Revisited

September 2, 2020

<u>Self-Care for Educators</u>

While fighting the good fight, protesting injustices, and demanding equality while also protecting ourselves in the midst of a global pandemic we have to remember to care for ourselves as educators. As educators, we not only have ourselves to consider, but we encounter hundreds of personalities daily. We come into contact with students, colleagues, administrators, and parents. We engage at a high level every single day for hours on end. The relationships we create while teaching are meaningful therefore we can be overcome with feelings of helplessness especially in such an uncertain time, as now.

Education has always been a constant. The academic calendar has been second nature in our society. September to June 8 AM - 3 PM, like clockwork. For our society, as well as for students, parents, and educators alike the school system has provided stability to our way of life. This shutdown has upended our sense of normalcy on a scale that is unprecedented.

As educators we have…
1.   Felt the loss of milestones like graduation, prom, end-of-year trips, and school traditions.

2.   Been empathetic to our students as they miss their classmates,

108

3. Felt unprepared to teach virtually.

4. Mourned illness and loss of life,

5. Managed our own homes at the same time as our own feelings.

This time off from "normal" only heightened the responses to the injustices that have been occurring in the Black community. Ahmaud Aubury. George Floyd. Breonna Taylor. Three names in a list of 100s that were wrongfully killed at the hands of law enforcement (or those pretending to be) because they were Black. The country reached a boiling point and many of us took a stand. Protests, peaceful and non-peaceful, sprung up all over evoking a cry for justice. A cry for help. As a black woman educator from Philly who teaches and counsels

Black and brown inner-city children every day, both circumstances combined affected me in ways that I could not have imagined. There has been a burden on us educators. It hurts. All of it. There are so many unknowns, and so many things wrong but many in education are natural helpers. We want to fix, teach, mold and do. This pandemic has impeded our ability to help in the ways we are accustomed to.

Here are a few tips that I have used to help me make sense of our current circumstances.

Have Self-Compassion

You are making the impossible possible. Treat yourself how you would someone else.

It's OK Not To Know

No one has all the answers, not even the teachers.

Know That This Is A Shared Experience

Many of us are tackling the same stresses. You don't have to carry the burden alone.

Take Care of the Basics

Get enough sleep, eat enough and more healthily, exercise, and drink enough water. Fuel your body so your basic survival tank doesn't run empty.

Feel Your Feelings

Remember that you are a person too. It is okay to feel it before you deal with it.

Unplug From Everything

Take a break from social media, the news, and TV.

Allow your brain time to decompress from all the access information.

Express Yourself

Get it out! Be creative! Draw, dance, write, talk. Find a way to release what is inside of you.

Educate Yourself About What Is Stressing You Out
Mad about racial injustices? Read articles about prison reform or police practices. Uncertain about teaching virtually? Sign up for a virtual learning webinar. Increase your knowledge base so you can feel more secure.

Make A Daily Schedule and Dedicated Workspace
This will free up mental space if you know what you are doing, when, and where each day.

Do Not Overbook Yourself

You don't have to be everywhere, doing everything at any time.

Just Be

Take time to sit and be still. Breathe. Do nothing. Take a moment to exist at the moment. Go inward if necessary or veg out on TV. We don't have to be super productive or "on" all the time. Be kind to yourself, educator. You cannot face this world ready to tackle the perils of COVID-19, racism, police brutality, gun violence, and virtual learning for your students and your own family on an empty tank. We're all in this together. Take care.

Journal Time: Speak To Me

Pick one of the above and elaborate on how you have used it to get through tough times.

_____

_____

_____

_____

_____

_____

_____

_____

_____

_____

September 15, 2020

A Forever Battle

Sometimes you need something to spark change. I often speak about self-care and life balance but have been slipping into a pattern of "Superwoman Dana saves the world" recently. I have not been good to myself at all.

I've been ignoring my body, not eating right, not drinking enough water, and not sleeping well. I've been running myself ragged behind the family. Stressing heavily at virtual work and just plain worrying myself sick. It's the beginning of the school year and as a teacher/counselor, I know how hard this time of year can be. Especially with balancing my own kids' schedules with my new set of students.

I have to take care of myself or there will be no me to take care of them. Some people may be thinking that I've said this before and they'd be right. This is a forever battle. I'm a caretaker at heart and those who identify as such will always have problems putting themselves first. I am evolving though. I know I have to do better, so I'm starting again right now.

September 26, 2020

<u>Breonna Taylor Revisited</u>

ARE WE EVEN SURPRISED?
DO WE EVEN MATTER?
THIS SYSTEM WAS NOT SET UP TO
PROTECT US. EMPOWER US.
POINT BLANK AND PERIOD.
SO WHAT DO WE DO NOW?
#BREONNATAYLOR

Do you know what that Breonna Taylor verdict verified? It proved that we have to do for ourselves. We have to matter for ourselves. We have to protect ourselves, whatever that means for you and yours. For me, it means that I have to continue to push. My girls have to reach their goals. I have to continue to show up for my students. They need to see my Black woman face running stuff behind the scenes. My husband needs me to encourage him in the background. My daughters need to be pushed to reach for their greatness. I need to remind my sister how amazing she is and of her wonderful abilities. I need to show up for myself. I have goals and dreams I still need to reach and I have to achieve them. I have to show up for myself. No one is coming to save us. They don't even care about us. But we got us. I'll make sure of it.

October 2020

"How can you be so hard on yourself when you show up as your best self every day? You're a warrior."

-Dana Martin

Entries
October 2nd: I Lost It
October 15th: Moon Talks
October 20th: Complex

October 2, 2020

I Lost It

Today I called out of work. I became too overwhelmed yesterday. I was so upset, emotionally drained and brain beat that I felt a panic attack approaching. I sat in a corner on the floor clutching my phone as I called my husband asking him to come home from work. I was a wreck, and my trigger wasn't terribly catastrophic, but it sent me over the edge.

The WI-FI wouldn't work properly. I work from home. Correction: I teach from home. There are kids in my face all day, on Zoom. My Zoom room is my classroom and my internet cutting out in the middle of the class is the equivalent of me walking out during a lesson and leaving the kids unattended. My internet cut out in the middle of class twice this week. Then it cut out completely in the middle of a meeting I was leading. That did it. The Zoom shut off, and my phone died while on the charger. My email wouldn't go through. Nothing would work all at the same time.

On top of this, both my kids were having trouble with the WI-FI too. Their frustration is palpable. I tried to keep it together for myself and them, but this week got harder and harder. I at least had my breakdown while I was home alone.

I felt so out of control. I called out of work for the next day saying I needed a mental health day. I called my husband and cried. He came and just sat with me. We tried to watch TV but the internet struck again. I was just emotionally drained and this was symbolic of everything happening all at the same time. Virtual teaching, limited social interaction, Breonna Taylor verdict, gun violence in Philly, this election, mail-in voting, and making decisions about every single simple thing is taxing. My brain hurt.

So I didn't work. I took a break from the computer for the day and did things that I felt I could control. I cleaned my house. I made balloon art. I assisted the girls with their schoolwork. I wrote. I read. I went grocery shopping. I cooked. I did things that were simple and felt like I took a little power back. I felt like I could start to make decisions again. I didn't feel crippled in submission.

So I went back to basics, my home, and my family. Forget self-care I had self-realization. I'm absolutely no good if I'm so wired. I can't do any of the jobs paid or at home. It's scary to keep coming back to this place of distress and figuring my way out of it. This anxiety-ridden world we are experiencing right now is revealing lessons every day.

October 15, 2020

Moon Talks

I am a moonchild. The energy from it flows directly to my center. It inspires me nightly. If I could talk to the moon I would say.

Dear Moon,

I could really use a pep talk. I don't understand all that's happening in this world right now and it's starting to wear me down. I'm finding myself searching for my purpose more and more. I'm struggling to adjust to this new normal, all these restrictions and safeguards. I want to feel freedom again. I miss your calming presence. You have a way of making the world make sense. I'm feeling lost.

Listening to the moon I'd hear it say...

Hey love,

Stop doing this to yourself. You create this space where you frustrate yourself and stress out. You already know how to solve your own problems, you just need a push to get going. You have all the power inside you. You're strong and built for these challenges. You know it and so do I. How can you be so hard on yourself when you show up as your best self every day? You're a warrior. Be kinder to yourself. Set your own goals. Start a new venture, write a new book. Nobody is coming to save you. Nobody cares so work harder. Do it. Whatever sets your soul on fire, because it is within you to succeed at whatever your heart desires. So get it together and tighten up.

I'd look up at the moon thankful for the motivating energy. For telling me what I already knew.

October 20, 2020

<u>Complex</u>

I'm full of contradictions, but so is everyone else. No one is linear, or one-way all the time. I am working my way through all of my intricacies and learning to accept myself the way I am. I find that I fall in love with things easily. I enjoy the feeling of liking something so much that it affects me deep down in my core. It's less stressful for me that way. With all my many titles I enjoy being so very different and representing so many different things. Politically I have very liberal beliefs and some conservative views as well.

As a wife, I am soft and submissive yet firm and boisterous in some areas. Financially I spend frivolously yet am overly consumed with saving money. Some students fear me, others adore me, and many others. I'm funny (like hilarious to myself!) but hella serious most times. I'm loud as hell and shy. I'm family-oriented but crave alone time. I yearn for stability yet spontaneity sets fire to my soul. I'm an adrenaline junkie but scared of high-stakes thrills. I believe it's possible to love two people at the same time. I believe in the 2nd amendment and gun safety/less gun access.

I want everything and nothing all at the same time. Crazy? No. Just human and that makes me complex. I watch social media posts roast people all the time for having seemingly contradictory views and actions.

Humans by nature are complex. It's not fair to judge people, period. People are complicated. Life is too.

November 2020

"Does my word really mean anything if I can't keep promises to myself?"

-Dana Martin

Entries

November 7th: Election
November 12th: Feel
November 22nd: Escape
November 28th: Boundaries

November 7, 2020

Election

Relief. I did not know that I had this much pent-up emotion surrounding this election. I honestly thought that we'd have four more years of the same administration. My body and mind have been so used to fear-mongering and hate that I am so turned off from my once beloved politics, but we won. I feel like that scene in Hamilton when they won the Revolutionary War. It seemed unlikely that we'd win simply because there has been so much hatred. It has been a hard four years but this election season, in particular, has hurt me.

I love political banter. I like to debate issues and possible solutions. I like to listen to debates and hear what candidates stand for and their platforms. This political season was so racked with hatred, untruths, and filth that I couldn't even bring myself to pay attention, especially with COVID-19 running rampant and Black people dying unjustly. It just felt unimportant and disconnected from what was really happening. This made me so sad, but I guess I held it all in because the sigh of relief I just took reached the core of my being. We won. Wow. Congrats, Joe. There's a Black woman a heartbeat away.

November 12, 2020

<u>Feel</u>

I get mad sometimes and that's okay. It took me a long time to be okay with my feelings. The way I used to process feelings was extreme. Either I was REALLY happy, EXTREMELY worried, WAY OVER THE TOP angry, or totally underwhelmed. Yeah, I know it sounds manic, but everything resonated with me. I'm still pretty emotional, but I have found a few ways to cope (writing being my favorite).

I talk about how I feel.

It took me a long time to realize that talking about things helps me to process them. When I'm angry, frustrated, or confused, being able to talk about a situation helps me see it clearer and move forward.

I sit with my feelings.

Every emotion doesn't need a reaction or even a name. Sometimes I get an overwhelming urge to smile out of nowhere and that's fine. I revel in those moments. Other times I get a negative feeling that I can't place so I sit still. Not worrying or trying to figure it out. I just notic the feeling and then let it go. The reason for the feeling usually comes to me once I've moved past it.

I don't put my feelings on people.

This one is harder than the others. My feelings are mine and mine alone. No one person can make me feel bad, sad, mad, upset, or any positive emotion for that matter. Situations and circumstances and my reaction to them cause me to feel a certain way. I'm big on not giving a person power over me and a good way to alleviate that stress is to not let someone control my feelings.

I am by no means perfect, but I have come a long way in this journey. I embrace how I feel all the time and I find that I am all the better for it.

November 22, 2020

<u>Escape</u>

Storytime. We took a much-needed family trip this past week and had so much fun! These restrictions and shutdowns have been taking a toll on each of us, especially the girls. They've been doing virtual elementary school and virtual college for the past nine months and dealing with this changing world just like everyone else and it has been trying to say the very least.

From mom virtual teaching and counseling to dad working outside the home every day and all of us pitching in every weekend to run the family business we were tired. Booking this trip gave us all something to look forward to. We needed warm weather and a break from the everyday. Taking strict precautions, we

traveled to San Juan, Puerto Rico, and enjoyed a very safe vacation. ATVs, mountains, rainforests, ocean breezes, kayaking, and resort-style living just for a short while helped break up the monotony of the everyday. This trip is exactly what we all needed. just peaceful. Just us.

We worked super hard every day and took a little time together to relax, rejoice, and reset. It was worth every minute.

November 28, 2020

<u>Boundaries</u>

Thanksgiving 2020 will go down as the year I needed to set and adhere to my own boundaries. I did not want to cook for Thanksgiving. This year has been stressful and full of weirdness and I just was not in the mood to do all of the things that go into a full Thanksgiving meal. I made this clear to my immediate and extended family. Also, we are still in the middle of the pandemic, and household gathering is semi-prohibited.

My hubby was on board as holidays are hard for him anyway. We were content finding a caterer or ordering Chinese for the night. Both of our girls had invitations to families' houses. Here's the thing, when others don't respect your "no", things can become complicated unnecessarily. I was guilted into cooking and attending a family Thanksgiving dinner. It really upset me. I did not want to attend but was made to feel guilty if I did not. It tanked my mood. I did not want to cook or leave my house, but here I was out of the house after cooking. This made me think of all the ways in which I do things that I do not want to do to spare the feelings of others. This isn't a dig at anyone in particular.

This is an examination of myself and how I failed to keep my word to myself. Does my word really mean anything if I can't keep my own promises? What do I really value? Do I value myself or pleasing others? I was

so upset with myself for not sticking to what I wanted to do. This is a recurring theme in my life, one which has led me in circles chasing my actual dreams. Le sigh. This pandemic really has me asking all the deep questions.

December 2020

"To miss someone is one of the most powerful feelings. Even in their physical absence, you long for their presence."

-Dana Martin

Entries

December 2nd: Ode To December 2nd

December 10th: The Other Essential Worker

December 17th: Loss. A Reflection

December 27th: Gun Violence As A Pandemic

December 31st: Finish Line

December 2, 2020

<u>Ode to December 2nd</u>

Ode to love on this December 2nd.

I love my hubby because he puts up with me volunteering him to move furniture to make my home office beautiful.

I love my kids because they give my life purpose, joy, and value. I'm a momager on so many levels.

I love my sister because she keeps me from having a big ego. No achievement too big for her to put me in check. Love my Nicole because talking to her makes me feel sane when all I feel is insanity.

Love my parents because they are my safety net. If anything fails they are there. They give us Martins something to aspire to.

And lastly, I love the memories that I have of my grandmother on what would have been her 91st birthday. Miss you to life.

My grandmother was indeed the traditional mother figure. She was a homemaker and cared for my sister and me while my parents worked. She would always have a solution for every problem. She had connections all over the neighborhood and knew someone who could be of assistance at the drop of a hat. My grandmother inspired my sense of wanting a community and of being a fixer. She was the center of our family, often being a beacon of hope for any lost soul. She never judged any of us, she was just always there for us. I strive to be like her in all these ways and she has influenced me to see the value in family ties and building a reliable trustworthy network of people who can help when needed.

For all this love on this day, I am thankful.

December 10, 2020

The Other Essential Workers

While virtually teaching my students a recurring theme plays out almost daily. Many of my students are working. Their work schedules interfere with their school schedules, and they are often front-line workers. When the pandemic forced statewide shutdowns of everything but essential businesses many of my students were already called to action. The businesses deemed essential were not only hospitals but also grocery stores, gas stations, discount stores, and fast-food restaurants. Family Dollar, Dollar General, Amazon, Walmart, and Target all are essential businesses and all employ teenagers, and where I live many of whom are Black and Brown.

As teachers we often hear students say they've missed online classes because of work, some will even join a Zoom class from behind the cash register at work. Numerous times this school year a student has been at work while in a virtual class. They are trying to balance completing assignments and being present in class while also bagging groceries and stocking shelves.

When full-time workers with children could no longer cover their shifts, my students could step in because attending school was no longer a prohibitive factor. When employees got ill and had to stay home, my students picked up more and more hours daily. When parents got sick and could not pull the full weight of supporting a household, some students would get multiple jobs to cover the gaps left by their parents.

With fewer extracurricular activities available they have more time to work. The jobs they have are necessary for our overall economy, as well as for our well-being. They come into contact with more people than average and thus are at a much greater risk of sickness, but are an unseen population. This is often an untold story. A story of a subset population of minority teens 16 - 20 who are working almost full-time hours due to high demand in this pandemic. Just shining a light on our youth in this pandemic. We don't want to overlook their sacrifices or undermine the risks they take to keep our economy running.

December 17, 2020

<u>Loss, A Reflection</u>

I am a helper. A lover. A fixer, but I can't fix everything, and the knowledge of this hit me hard this year. I've been mourning the loss of relationships over and over again.

And it hurts.

Unexpected endings hurt.
Even when the decision was mutual. It hurts.
Even losing toxic energy can be painful.
Or growing distant gradually.
When the loss was for my own good, it hurt badly. When a life suddenly ended, it devastated.
Missing a person's energy and laughter, their demeanor and spirit hurt. And I've been powering through hurt this year.

A few endings sent me into a sadness that I didn't even realize was there. The impact people have on you can go unnoticed until you no longer have access to them.

To miss someone is one of the most powerful feelings. Even in their physical absence, you long for their presence.

No matter how much sense it makes for the separation. No matter the rhyme or reason. No matter how much better off my present circumstance is without them. No matter if it's supported by a series of hard decisions and conviction. It still hurts. It really hurts.

The fact that I cannot fix it hurts my feelings.

I've been in mourning for the loss of my relationship. Things just won't be the same.

But even though I'm resigned to the fact that these relationships are gone, I'm still in the background waiting for a chance to reconcile, to love again, to laugh again, to feel again.

The duality is not lost on me.

December 27, 2020

<u>Gun Violence As A Pandemic</u>

The pandemic that most affect my life is gun violence. The number of people that have been shot or killed or affected by gun violence is more than I know that have been affected by Covid-19. Every time I turn on the

news another person is reported shot and dead. I"m always checking the location to see if I know anyone

living close by. I'm fearful all the time of getting a phone call or a text message that someone I know has been shot and killed. It hurts to feel like I'm in constant fear. Every

day I'm scared to death and kids are normalizing death.

It is unfair. The value of life is diminishing. People now know what to do whenever someone dies.

Candlelight vigils.
Balloon releases.
Funeral procession.
Repast.
Food for the
family. T-shirts.
Teddy bears.
Cardboard cutouts.
Memorial service.
Burial.
Hashtags and social media RIP tributes.
Updated profile pics and bios.

It feels like our lives have so little value. What makes it even worse is that the murder clearance rate in my city is abysmal and even worse for people of color. There is

little hope that my murder will be solved because I"m

a person of color living in a Black neighborhood in Philly, sadly. I truly feel this way. It scares me to think that if I were killed that those close to me would mourn and then the world would simply move on. Over the course of this year, the cases of murder and gunshot victims have increased exponentially. There is so little

value tied to someone"s life. There is so much time on

people's hands. This issue hits me hard because I love

the population of people that are most affected, 16 through 30-year-old Black people. Male and female alike. I have a daughter in this age range. I have family in this age range. I counsel this age range. Most if not all of the students I have ever taught are in this age range. I am in fear that I will get a phone call that someone else I care for, someone I've loved, liked, or encountered has been killed by gunfire. Unfortunately, this does not feel like a priority in this city. Preventing gun violence does not seem to be a priority. It feels like if you are Black, young, from the city, God forbid poor if you are shot no one will care. Your murder will likely not be solved. That is what has been demonstrated over and over again.

I'm making observations, not placing blame. This pandemic has reduced activities for people to engage in fruitful jobs, school, and extracurricular activities and as a result, there is much more idol time. There has been an increase in money from the government such as pandemic unemployment, forgivable business loans, drugs are easier to come by, and guns are more readily available. Policing is affected by the Black Lives Matter Movement, with more citizens using video to protect their rights and more accountability measures. People are less focused on the community and more focused on individuals. Throw in the mental health effects of living through a global pandemic that has changed everyone's livelihood and you have the basis of an epidemic of violence. But what can be done?

I'm scared a lot. Just because so many things can happen to anyone, I hold dear. The feeling never gets better. To hear about the death of a person young or old by gun violence is never something I can get used to. This is the issue of our time, of our city, of our youth. At this point, Philadelphia is approaching 500 homicides this year with over 2,000 shootings. This will be the highest in 30 years. This needs to be attacked in the same manner as the COVID-19 pandemic. **THIS IS A CRISIS.**

December 31, 2020

<u>Finish Line</u>

I feel like I've been clawing my way to the finish line for the past 10 months. Different. This year has been the most different experience of my life. Unexpected, unprecedented, just downright scary. I'm sitting here on the last day of the year grateful to have my health and sanity. I am happy to have my loved ones and home. I am happy to be able to provide. I fought my way to winter break. Even virtually there was work that needed to be done.

I felt strange trying to adhere to college application deadlines with the world seemingly on fire everywhere. I planned a virtual school event to help take my mind off how bad I felt about this holiday season. The holidays usually bring me so much joy but I was hurting for my students. The lack of physical interaction was apparent in all online interactions with kids. Adults too. We were all just trying to make it to winter break and when it came we could finally rest. Not having to log into a computer for the last week has given me a pause I didn't realize I needed. I was sick of that computer. Downright sick of it. Sick of Zoom, sick of school systems, sick of Google Drive, and sick of emails. My world has been reduced to a screen and I hate hate hate it, but at least it's something. I have a job when so many others do not and

I am grateful to still interact with my kids even if it"s not physically. I did not shop for one Christmas gift until December 23rd. I'm always a late shopper, but this year was so strange. Time is a construct that just did not adhere to me this year and I looked up and it was Christmas Eve. At least I planned my gifts out and had a strategy for gifting. It helped that most stores were curbside pickup.

Christmas Day though changed my life. Even though the day started late for us and a storm knocked out internet and phone service for most of the day we gathered around the tree when everyone woke up and exchanged gifts. Before the girls opened their gifts they gave us both gifts that they bought with their own money. They were so happy to get us things that we both wanted. I cried when I opened my gifts. I was surprised, and I'm never surprised. I usually know what's in every box in my house and the notes they wrote brought me to tears. Sometimes I forget that they are watching me just like I watch them.

My hubby and I spent time together as tradition and the day was beyond amazing. I couldn't have asked for a better Christmas in a year of crazy. I've relaxed hard this last week. Tried to stay in the house as much as possible. It has felt like I've been running constantly to get here, but I don't know why. It's not like at midnight everything will return to normal. It just feels like something will happen. So as I approach the finish line of 2020, the year that kept on giving and taking I say this to myself. You survived. Well done.

Life Lessons

Like us all, 2020 has taught me much. The uncertainty, fear, joys and triumphs have brought me a new sense of self, a new sense of being. The recurring lessons that came each and every month have been hard yet necessary. Here are some of the lessons I gleaned from my year of realization.

My Lessons Learned

I Create My Own Reality.

What is for me will be for me. The issues that I experienced in life prior to this incredibly transformative year simply do not have the same impact. I choose where my focus goes. I choose what has power over me. I choose whom I give attention. I choose what occupies my attention. I am an emotional person by nature. I believe in expressing myself but have become much more reserved in my outward responses. I do not like to give away my power. I am not saying that I have control over every aspect of my life, I am simply saying that I choose how I respond to what happens to me. I cannot change what is happening in the world, but I can control my reaction therefore I control my reality.

The Same Test Will Repeat Itself Until The Lesson Is Learned

My health and mental stability were tested over and over again. Self-care was a recurring theme throughout my year. Self-preservation. I came back to the same lesson repeatedly because I was not doing the work necessary for myself. I failed to learn it the first, second, or third time, so it returned repeatedly. Pay attention to yourself. Your mind, body, and spirit know what it needs and when. If you fail to do the work on yourself you will be in a constant struggle with yourself.

Who"s Here Is Supposed To Be Here

Presence matters. Those who choose to be a presence in your life are supposed to be there. This time of introspection has helped me reevaluate those I choose to offer my presence to and likewise, those who choose to give me theirs. Communication and interactions were less frequent in 2020 outside of my immediate family. Arrangements had to be made to spend time with people. Those who showed up in my life thought about me enough to make the effort. Those that I encountered this year I thought of and initiated contact with.

The lesson is this; if they want to be in my life they will, if they do not, they will not, and vice versa. Death came in droves this year. I'm spending my days cultivating an atmosphere sans awkward encounters, guessing intentions, and mind games.

Things can change, quickly.

This lesson goes without saying, especially in 2020. There was a buzz about a new virus and then the world was shut down by week's end. Things changed at the drop of a hat. Low-income kids with little access to technology was thrust into the digital age. Money was found for laptops and internet access for millions of families in record time. Food became scarce for people who had limited resources. Lines became longer. Things became less convenient. There were massive protests and calls for large-scale justice, which people actually paid attention to. People were forced to stop the unnecessary and unessential things and stay home. Lives were being taken by COVID-19 and violence every day. Nothing seemed stable. Virtual became the norm in a world where gathering and community reign supreme. Secure jobs became unsecured and even for those of us who were lucky enough to remain employed, there were risks involved. Constant decisions had to be made whether to risk health to get a paycheck, to dumb down the school curriculum and pass every student, to go outside to the store, or to invite a delivery person to your home. Hard choices had to be made almost hourly. With no correct answers. The only answer is that change can will, and did come. and it will continue to.

Everything doesn't matter.

You can't survive keeping too many things in high priority. Everything cannot have the same level of importance. In 2020 there were so many issues and causes happening at once that caring too much about one could pull you from another. While it is quite human to be able to engage in multiple perspectives and have duplicity and contradictory interests the high-stakes nature of the reigning issues of 2020 can in and of themselves be all consuming. Pick your battles. Pick what's important. Everything can not matter.

Love myself in this moment

Giving grace has a whole new meaning after the year we just had. I have chosen to love myself just the way I am currently. I gained weight and lost my sense of self. I fell into a depression and dealt with anxiety. I questioned my worth repeatedly, but you know what? I survived. I survived the darkest days. I am still alive and in my right mind and that in and of itself is good enough for me. I love who I am and who I am becoming. I am stronger than I ever knew and that person deserves to be loved.

Get ready

This final lesson is the most profound for me. Get ready. I was living my life as if I had time. More time to waste, but I simply do not. As cliche as the saying, "tomorrow is not promised" rings true. I have lost people to both death and life this year. Money became illusive. I suddenly found myself with all the time in the world that I had wished for and I was unprepared. My finances weren't ready for a catastrophe. My house wasn't ready for a stay-at-home order. My relationships were not ready for extended time spent. My businesses weren't ready to increase or decrease. My body wasn't ready to be so still. I was not ready. Most of us weren't. I always asked for a break to rest and get things in order. Well, listen, I got my break yet nothing was orderly. I have now learned that I need to be ready for the unexpected.

This life is a gift. I've always known this, but living through the year 2020 has shown me how precious our life is and can be. I am the master of my destiny. My power lies in my hands. How I choose to show up is on me and honey I'm showing up for myself over and over again.

October 2021

Epilogue

My kids aren't afraid of Covid-19. They're afraid of getting shot. There have been 432 murders in Philadelphia as of October 12 2021 with over 1700 people shot this year. Gun violence is rampant in the communities in which the kids I teach live as well as in my own. I am fearful of getting another message that someone I know has been shot and killed daily. I check my phone each morning hoping that my students and family members have made it through another night in Philly. Prayers of protection are abundant.

The pandemic and the subsequent shutdown have created an alternate universe where money is both scarce and more easily available, guns are easier to get, drug overdoses are higher than ever, social media beefs result in deaths, jobs are both in abundance yet not for everyone, social interactions are more high stakes and a structured day is less important. There's a sense of heightened agitation prevalent in our communities layered with a feeling of despair.

"I want to leave Philly because it's not safe." This is a direct quote from a high school senior who just wants to make it to see his next birthday. What troubles me is that

153

the communities most impacted by violence in this city are Black and Brown, between the ages of 15 and 30, and live in communities hit hardest by poverty and crime. Resources to improve one's trajectory may be available but the information isn't always reaching target populations. There are career programs, financial workshops, job training, college fairs, GED programs, food banks, and community resources, but those they are meant for aren't accessing them. There seems to be a disconnect between the resources available and the intended recipients.

"If I get shot the person who did it won't get caught." Another quote, another kid who doesn't feel supported, seen, or valued. Less than 20% of murders are solved in Philly right now. That's a 4 in 5 chance of getting away with it. Good odds if you want to kill someone. The perception is that no one looks for the murderer of a young Black person or of a person who lives in a certain neighborhood. Add race and class to it and the case is likely to go unsolved permanently. It can feel unfair and demoralizing to feel invalidated by a place you call home.

"Why is the missing girl in Wyoming getting all this press? There are girls missing here and no one cares. My cousin got shot and no one was investigated. No one came to the house and asked questions. There were no news cameras, no police or detectives. Why are we different?" Another kid, another quote, another person feeling like they don't matter in the place they live. They see the double standard and feel helpless.

From working with Philly young adults for almost 20 years I know that feeling valuable in their environment goes a long way; feeling respected goes a long way. When Philly officials simply tell what they are doing to curb violence and describe the money being spent on programs to ensure the public's safety from afar it doesn't translate. Where is the state of emergency? Where are the town watches or guardian angels? Where is the community mobilization? Where are the law students to help police officials with unsolved crimes? Where are the tech innovators to invest in our community centers and cameras for our neighborhoods? Where are the state-of-the-art capital ventures to improve the quality of life in the communities directly impacted by gun violence and death?

Don't tell us things are happening when every single day someone is killed and the murder is likely to go unsolved. It's hard to trust those in charge when they don't have the same stake in the game. They don't live in the communities. They don't work in the communities. They aren't personally losing people and dealing with those left behind.

COVID-19 has impacted all of us, but gun violence has impacted me, my family, and my students far more closely and immediately. Our kids need more from us as the City of Philadelphia. We can play the blame game all we want:

"Parents need to supervise their kids"
"Kids need to show respect to adults"
"People need to go to work and not hang out."

"Guns aren't the answer. They need to learn how to solve problems better."
"People should call the police to report crime."

"Kids shouldn't hang outside or on the corners during the day or late at night."
"People should tell on those committing the crimes so they can be off the street."

All those are statements I've heard from adults in the communities, during press conferences, from fellow teachers, Philly politicians, and public figures. Here's the thing though, placing blame does not solve the problems. This is an emergency. The feeling of safety is a basic human right that many of us are being robbed of. It feels as if no one cares until it impacts them directly. That's not fair to those in our city who need us to step up.

Acknowledgments

When I started writing this book I experienced the loss of life. At the beginning of 2020, I was mourning the loss of two young men. Tysheem Pennock who passed away at 20 years old and Suhail Gillard, a student in my class, lost his life at the age of 18, in the middle of his senior year. As I embarked on this writing journey their deaths impacted me. As the year went on death continued. Nashid Al-Hadi, whom I met through his sister, passed in the spring at the age of 23 whose death felt personal. Laron Welcome's death came in the summer of 2020 and hurt like hell for his loved ones.

At this time I kept evaluating why death was coming in what felt like droves. On the last day of 2020, Diyaan Smith was killed. He was 16, a student whose family I'd grown to love. As I began editing and revising another student Justin Porter was killed in early 2021. Another teen. Watching the impact of these deaths wreak havoc on our community was transformational. Two beloved fathers passed away in the fall of 2021. David Mitchell and Carlton Price, Sr. were the steadfast patriarchs of their families, strong examples of Black husbands and fathers.

Right before publishing at the start of 2022 my brother-in-law Curtis McKnight was killed in a hit-and-run accident. This sucked the life out of us. Words can't describe the impact that his loss had on my husband and our entire family. I put this book out into the universe as a tribute to each of these souls who are mourned by thousands. I chose to dedicate my book to them because their lives matter to those who loved and knew them. It is my prayer that they rest in peace with the knowledge that those of us left behind will continue to carry on in their wake.

Thank you, Lord, for giving me the strength and wisdom to give this story to the world. Your love compassion and favor for me have been shown every day of my life.

Tyrec, you are the epitome of love and support. Our love and partnership have made this marriage so worth it. I thank you for believing in me. Thanks for being the rock to my kite. You keep me grounded baby. I love you.

Jaleya and Melody, my not-so-little daughters. Live your life! Don't wait until the moment is right. I want you to believe that you can do anything. Seriously. This world is what you make it. Don't lay scared. you both are my inspiration and I love you deeply and truly.

To my sister Deannalee. You keep me in check and I appreciate that. I always knew there was someone watching that I needed to take care of. You are wonderful just the way you are. believe it. you are my sunshine, always. Love Bunny

Debbie and Danny aka Mommy and Daddy, I love you beyond words. I'm a true daddy's girl with my momma's attitude you raised me to be who I am. smart, funny, kind, responsible, and full of love. Your example and life lessons have infiltrated my adult life. My family mirrors the one I grew up with! Seriously, my husband and dad are like twins! I love you both. Without you, I would not be. Thank you for everything you've ever done for me.

Nicole, I could not do most of what I do without you in my corner. You have literally saved my life on multiple occasions. There is no scenario where you are not a part of my world. Your love and constant encouragement helped me do the impossible. Thank you for always being exactly what I need.

To my publisher, Brandi Hester-Harrell of Mahogany Pen Publishing thank you for your patience and assistance with all the behind-the-scenes. I know I'm a visionary and a procrastinator and that made your job hard but look at what we've done!

My editor Karissa. You are phenomenal! Thank you for the time and consideration in making this book ready for the public. I appreciate your notes and patience in this process.

To every student past and present with whom I have had an impact. There are far too many to name, but I thrive off your collective spirit. I am better because I was your teacher and counselor. Remember that always.

To my extended family and friends. Thank you for always seeing something in me. From being the skinny light-skinned smart kid to the know-it-all young adult with a smart mouth and attitude to match you have supported me in my countless endeavors. I truly do not take your support for granted. Thank you all from the bottom of my heart.

About the Author

Dana Martin is an accomplished writer, and educator in Philadelphia. With over 15 years of experience in college counseling and teaching, she empowers students and families on their educational journeys. Dana's powerful writings focus on embracing life's struggles and finding inspiration in adversity. She shares valuable insights on college access, parenting, navigating Black experiences, urban teen issues, and more.

As a respected college advisor, Dana has guided thousands of students through college preparation, applications, and financial aid management. She is a sought-after speaker on college access issues and has been featured in various media outlets. In addition to her writing, Dana currently serves as an Assistant Principal, driving a school wide postsecondary culture and also organizes pre college workshops and college tours for local organizations. She currently serves as the Director of Education for For Black Girls Online.

With a rich educational background, Dana is a proud Central High School and Temple University graduate. Her passion for connecting people and college counseling drives her to make a lasting impact on students' lives.

Contact:
www.danaleemartin.com
danamartinwriter@gmail.com